To Drew, Daniele and Suz

Typeset in Century Schoolbook.
The illustrations in this book are created by hand
and digitally colored.
Manufactured in Hong Kong.

Library of Congress Cataloging-in-Publication Data
Frazier, Craig, 1955-
  Stanley goes fishing / Craig Frazier.
    p. cm.
Summary: Stanley, a fellow who looks at life differently, goes on a
fishing trip and discovers that the fish are not where they should be.
  ISBN-13: 978-0-8118-5244-9 (13-digit)
  ISBN-10: 0-8118-5244-X (10-digit)
  [1. Fishing–Fiction. 2. Fish–Fiction.] I. Title.
  PZ7.F869Ss 2006
  [E]–dc22
2005012807

Distributed in Canada by Raincoast Books
9050 Shaughnessy Street, Vancouver, British Columbia, V6P 6E5

10 9 8 7 6 5 4 3 2 1

Chronicle Books LLC
85 Second Street, San Francisco, California, 94105

www.chroniclekids.com

STANLEY

Goes Fishing

Craig Frazier

chronicle books · san francisco

Early one morning, Stanley had just one thing on his mind...

...going fishing.

Stanley put his boat in the
water. He had everything
he needed.

He rowed up the curly stream looking for the perfect place.

When he found it, Stanley cast his line into the deep blue water.

He waited patiently.

Suddenly, he felt a huge
tug on his line.

He could tell that he had
hooked something big.

It was big, but it wasn't exactly
what he was hoping for.

Stanley had an idea.

Stanley caught a fish.
Then another and another.

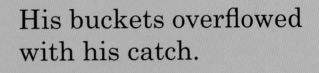

His buckets overflowed
with his catch.

Then, Stanley dumped all the fish into the stream.

He turned his boat back home.
It had been Stanley's best day of
fishing ever...

...and the fish's too.